Sebastian,

May your life be
with blessings! Congratulations
on this special day. We love you!
Zavien Family

For Adeline
—Matthew

For Sam and Leo
—Kimberley

When I Pray for You

Hardcover ISBN 978-0-525-65058-4
eBook ISBN 978-0-525-65061-4

Text copyright © 2019 by Matthew Paul Turner
Illustrations copyright © 2019 by Kimberley Barnes

Cover design by Mark D. Ford; cover illustration by Kimberley Barnes; cover type design by Liss Amyah

Published in the United States by WaterBrook, an imprint of the Crown Publishing Group, a division of Penguin Random House LLC, New York.

WATERBROOK® and its deer colophon are registered trademarks of Penguin Random House LLC.

Library of Congress Cataloging-in-Publication Data
Names: Turner, Matthew Paul, 1973– author.
Title: When I pray for you / Matthew Paul Turner.
Description: First edition. | Colorado Springs : WaterBrook, an imprint of the Crown Publishing Group, a division of Penguin Random House LLC, 2019.
Identifiers: LCCN 2018018133| ISBN 9780525650584 (hardcover) | ISBN 9780525650614 (ebook)
Subjects: LCSH: Parents—Religious life. | Intercessory prayer—Christianity.
Classification: LCC BV4529 .T93 2019 | DDC 248.8/45—dc23
LC record available at https://lccn.loc.gov/2018018133

Printed in the United States of America
2019

10 9 8 7 6 5 4

SPECIAL SALES
Most WaterBrook books are available at special quantity discounts when purchased in bulk by corporations, organizations, and special-interest groups. Custom imprinting or excerpting can also be done to fit special needs. For information, please email specialmarketscms@penguinrandomhouse.com or call 1-800-603-7051.

When I Pray for You

Matthew Paul Turner illustrated by **Kimberley Barnes**
Author of *When God Made You*

WATERBROOK

From the moment I saw you,
I started to pray.

Big prayers and small ones
I have sent God's way.

I prayed as I held you
when you sat in my lap.

I prayed while we rocked,
as you peacefully napped.

As you took your first steps
and when you started to run.

As I pushed you on swing sets
or we skipped in the sun.

I prayed you felt safe,
full of joy and content.

That when I whispered "I love you,"
you knew what I meant.

When you said your first word,
repeating what you'd heard.

When you mooed like a cow
or tweeted like a bird.

When you giggled out loud
or made yourself proud.

To God I said "Thank you,"
and to you I said "Wow."

As I watched you pretend,

all alone or with friends,

I prayed over you again and again.

'Cause when I pray for you,
God knows this is true,

every word I whisper
is a prayer for me too.

At the moment I hear you jump out of bed,
I start praying that God puts good thoughts in your head.

I pray when you're smiling and when you feel sad.
I pray when you're sick, embarrassed, or mad.

When you're kicking a ball
or twirling in place.

When I know what you're thinking
by the look on your face.

I pray you grow strong, have passion and fight.
And stand up for what's good with all of your might.

I pray Heaven protects you, that you're generous and kind.
That your brave little spirit never ceases to shine.

That you believe in yourself and follow what's true.
That your confidence grows just as fast as you do.

As I drive you to school.

While you splash in a pool.

As you challenge a friend to a lightsaber duel.

When you open your eyes to a birthday surprise.
When the joy on your face cannot be disguised.

I pray you love well.

That the light in you swells.

That the story God writes is the one that you tell.

'Cause when I pray for you, I imagine God's view.
And pray all that God sees comes alive inside you.

When suddenly it seems you've gotten so tall.
When you've grown up so much that my lap's way too small.
When you're glued to a screen or your bedroom's unclean.
When you're no longer a child but not yet a teen.

I'll pray when you're hyper,
obnoxious, or chill.

I'll pray when you're chatty
and cannot sit still.

When you're running relays
or performing school plays.

Or you're somewhere in the middle of a garage-band phase.

When you know all the answers
or just think that you do.

When you find out the hard way
you know less than you knew.

I'll pray you choose hope should you ever face fear.
And seek wisdom with patience when the pathway's unclear.

That you will love others, whether strangers or friends,
with the same kind of love that God feels for them.

When you break from your shell
to stand up for yourself
and I realize you didn't ask me for my help,

I'll pray and I'll cheer.
(I'll probably shed a tear.)
And hope that you know, if you need me, I'm here.

'Cause when I pray for you,

no matter what we go through,

the dreams that you dream,

I'll be dreaming them too.

At the moment you realize
it's time to explore,

I'll pray God gives you wings
and, like an eagle, you'll soar.

I'll pray where you go,
that wherever you land,
you'll find purpose and meaning and a role in God's plan.

That you'll know who you are.
And like what you do.
And love yourself fully, as God wants you to.

I'll pray you keep shining.

That God keeps refining.

That your story reflects what in you God's designing.

That you'll give and you'll share
with compassion and care.
That how you live life will, to God, be a prayer.

'Cause when I pray for you,

I pray all that you do

brings love and brings light,

and helps the world shine like new.